Purple Class
and the Skelington

For Mandy, Nicky, Gavin and Helen

Sean Taylor

Purple Class and the Skelington

and other stories

**Illustrated
by Helen Bate**

F

FRANCES LINCOLN
CHILDREN'S BOOKS

Purple Class and the Skelington copyright © Frances Lincoln Limited 2006
Text copyright © Sean Taylor 2006
Illustrations copyright © Helen Bate 2006
Cover illustration copyright © Polly Dunbar 2006

First published in Great Britain and in the USA in 2006 by
Frances Lincoln Children's Books, 4 Torriano Mews,
Torriano Avenue, London NW5 2RZ

www.franceslincoln.com

Distributed in the USA by Publishers Group West

British Library Cataloguing in Publication Data
available on request

ISBN 10: 1-84507-377-0
ISBN 13: 978-84507-377-0

Printed in the United Kingdom

3 5 7 9 8 6 4 2

Contents

Purple Class
and the Skelington

7

The Wild Area

28

Slinkypants,
the Crazy Snake

45

The Green Lady

65

Purple Class
and the Skelington

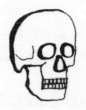

As Jamal hung up his bag in the corridor there was a glint in his eye. He was at school extra early. He had remembered his reading book. It looked as if it was going to be one of his good mornings. Then Zina came rushing round the corner.

"Jamal!" she said, "Mr Wellington's dead!"

"What?" asked Jamal.

"Mr Wellington's dead!" repeated Zina.

Jamal felt a bit fed-up. On the very day he'd managed to get to school extra early and remember his reading book, his teacher had to go and die.

"We've got to tell Mrs Sammy!" blurted out Zina.

They hurried down the corridor to the head-teacher's office.

"Mrs Sammy! Miss!" called Zina. "Mr Wellington's dead!"

Mrs Sammy raised her eyebrows. "Sorry," she said, "I've got Mr Furlong banging holes in the ceilings and a school inspector arriving. I haven't got time for jokes!" But then she looked at their faces and realized it wasn't a joke. "Well, where is he dead?" she asked.

"In his chair," said Zina.

Mrs Sammy got up and walked down the corridor. There, in his raincoat, unlocking the door into Purple Class, was Mr Wellington. Mrs Sammy breathed out.

"He looks alive to me!" she said.

Zina seemed slightly disappointed. "Well there's someone dead in there," she said.

"Mr Wellington," said Mrs Sammy, "is there someone dead in your classroom? Yes or no?"

"Yes and no," said Mr Wellington.

Mrs Sammy poked her head through the doorway.

"There!" said Zina.

Sitting on Mr Wellington's chair was a skeleton.

"Oh," said Mrs Sammy.

"It's not real, is it?" asked Jamal.

"It's a model," said Mr Wellington, walking across the carpet and tapping the skeleton's skull. "We're going to use it to learn all about bones."

"Well I wish you'd hang it on its stand," suggested Mrs Sammy.

"Just about to," Mr Wellington nodded, wheeling a white stand out of the stationery cupboard.

"Zina thought it was you," said Jamal.

"It doesn't look anything like me," said Mr Wellington.

"It does," smiled Zina.

The bell went and Mr Wellington fetched the rest of the class from the playground. As they came in and sat on the carpet, everybody started chattering about the skeleton.

"Right! Good morning," said Mr Wellington. "Who had a good weekend?"

Lots of hands went up.

"I spent some quality time with our new puppy," said Ivette. "She's called Dolly."

"Lucky Dolly," smiled Mr Wellington.

"I wish we had a puppy," said Jodie. "My dad's got a pet snake."

"A snake?" said Mr Wellington. "What's that called?"

"Slinkypants," said Jodie.

Everyone laughed.

"That's a funny name!" grinned Leon.

"My dad's a funny bloke," shrugged Jodie.

Mr Wellington started taking the register. As he did, a great banging came from up above the classroom.

"What's that?" asked Shea.

Mr Wellington explained that Mr Furlong, the caretaker, was repairing hot-water pipes in the roof, so he would be making noise all morning.

He finished taking the register. The class went to sit at their tables and Mr Wellington walked over to the skeleton.

"Now, who knows what this is?"

"My auntie after she did the F-Plan Diet," said Shea.

"It's a skelington," said Zina.

"A *skeleton*," said Mr Wellington.

"It's a human skeleton," added Ivette.

"That's right," said Mr Wellington. "You've got all these bones inside you."

"Uuuuuuurgh!" said Yasmin and Jodie.

Ivette put up her hand and asked, "Have we got the skeleton because the school inspector's coming?"

"No," said Mr Wellington, "but in case anyone's forgotten, Mr Gates, the school inspector, is coming to our lesson after break. So concentrate now. When he comes, you can show him how much you've learnt."

Mr Wellington told Yasmin to hand out the

science books. He gave everyone a diagram of a skeleton to cut out and glue in. When they had finished, they sat on the carpet and he told them to listen carefully. As he wheeled the skeleton to the front of the class all the children edged away from it. No one wanted it to touch them, and Leon said he heard it whisper something.

"What did it whisper?" asked Mr Wellington.

"Roasted peanuts," said Leon.

Jamal said it had whispered something to him as well, and Mr Wellington put his hands on his hips.

"What did it say to you, Jamal? *Two packets of cheese and onion crisps, please?*"

Mr Wellington explained to the class that the human body contains 206 bones. He told them about the skull. Then he undid a clip so that the skeleton's skull opened like a box.

"Uuuuuuurgh!" said Yasmin and Jodie.

"Shhh!" said Mr Wellington, closing it again.

He told them about the main leg bones: the femur, the tibia and the fibula. He said each name and got different children to repeat them. When he stood up, Ivette screamed and all her friends screamed as well.

"QUIET!" shouted Mr Wellington. "What is it, Ivette?"

"The skeleton moved its eyes!" said Ivette.

"It hasn't even got eyes," said Mr Wellington.

"I know," said Ivette. "It moved the holes where its eyes should be."

All the class gasped in horror.

"It's looking at Jodie," said Shea.

Jodie grabbed hold of Mr Wellington's leg. Mr Wellington shouted in his angriest voice, "QUIET! LOOK! IT'S NOT A REAL SKELETON!" He shook the model so that it rattled. "It's made of plastic," he said. "It can't say *roasted peanuts* to Leon. It can't look at Jodie. It can't do anything. Look! You can wave its arms around. You can dance with it."

He put one arm around the skeleton's waist, stretched out its right hand and started dancing. The children laughed.

"See?" smiled Mr Wellington, "It's just a model." A few heads nodded. "Good. Well, it's nearly time for break. Tidy things up! And when Mr Gates comes in after break I want you to remember what I've been telling you."

***

The bell rang. Mr Wellington sent the class out to the playground but, almost at once, a shower of rain came down.

"All right!" called Mr Wellington. "Back you come! It's going to be a wet-break! Ivette, get the games and puzzles down from the wet-break shelf. I'm going to have a coffee. Miss Zanetos is next door in Orange Class so NO silliness!"

Out he went, leaving the door ajar. Jamal opened a packet of Hula-Hoops. He ate a few, then put one on to the skeleton's finger like a ring. Zina was sitting on a table, eating an apple. She watched as Jamal lifted up the skeleton's finger and put it in the hole where its nose should be.

"The skeleton's picking its nose!" he said.

Zina laughed so much that a bit of her apple fell on the floor.

Shea came over. He took the skeleton's other

hand, reached it up on top of the skull and said, "'That's how Mr Wellington scratches his head!'"

"No," said Zina, opening the skeleton's mouth and pushing her apple inside. "That's how Jamal eats."

Everyone was laughing now. Miss Zanetos would have heard if Mr Furlong hadn't been banging about in the roof.

Then Jamal bent down and started wiggling the skeleton by the hips. "Move… move… move your *baarrdy!!!*" he sang.

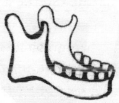

The skeleton's hands flew up and down and its feet kicked backwards and forwards. It looked so funny dancing with the apple in its mouth that Shea almost fell over laughing. The louder people laughed, the faster Jamal shook. Then there was a pinging sound and the model flew off its stand. The skull spun off. The children gasped. The rest of the skeleton lurched on to Mr Wellington's chair, whacking an arm against Jamal's head and scattering bones across the tables.

"Mr Wellington said no silliness," said Yasmin.

"I didn't mean to do it," said Jamal, standing with one of the leg-bones in his hand.

There was a mad rush to pick up the bones. Leon found a hand in the basin and Yasmin found a toe in the plant pot. Jamal managed to put together the rib cage and hang it back on the stand.

"This is the spine," said Jodie, holding up one of the arms.

"That's a leg!" said Leon.

"A leg doesn't have a hand," said Zina.

They managed to put together a leg. But when they put the arms on, one of them was twice as long as the other. And that was when Mr Wellington came in.

"I've just seen Mr Gates," he said. "He'll be along shortly." Then he noticed the skeleton. "WHAT'S GOING ON NOW?" he roared.

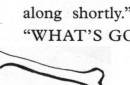

***

"It wasn't just me," said Jamal.

"I'll find out who it was later," snapped Mr Wellington. "Right now I want this skeleton fixed. Look, the ribs are upside down! And it's only got one leg!"

"Here's the skull," said Shea, handing it to Mr Wellington.

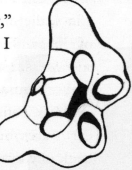

"It's got an apple in its mouth! Who put that there?" Mr Wellington tried to pull the apple out but the teeth kept snapping at his fingers.

Then Zina whispered from the doorway, "Mr Grapes is coming."

"What?" said Mr Wellington, fixing the skull on to the spine with the apple still in its mouth. "Mr Gates?"

"He's coming down the corridor," said Zina.

"Well, we can't let him see this," hissed Mr Wellington. "Shea and Jamal, wheel it out into the playground."

Shea and Jamal wheeled the wonky skeleton over to the door into the playground. Everyone else sat at their tables. A moment later, Mr Gates tapped on the door and walked in.

Outside, Shea and Jamal pushed the skeleton as fast as they could. When they went past Orange Class, the children inside could only see the top of it bobbing past the window, jiggling its shoulders. For a moment they were silent. Then they screamed.

Miss Zanetos threw open the door. "What on earth are you boys doing?" she said. "Take that back to your classroom!"

"But Miss Zanetos, we're…" started Jamal.

"TAKE THAT BACK TO YOUR CLASSROOM, FULL STOP!" shouted Miss Zanetos.

"All right, sorry," said Jamal, and he turned the skeleton round. As it jiggled past Orange Class its jaw dropped open and the apple fell out. The children screamed even louder.

Back in Purple Class, Mr Wellington raised his eyebrows. "Sounds like fun next door!"

"Yes," smiled Mr Gates. "Now, what will you be doing this lesson?"

"The human skeleton," said Mr Wellington.

"Fine," said Mr Gates. "May I glance through your lesson plans?"

Mr Wellington nodded. "They're in the stationery cupboard. I'll fetch them for you in just a moment."

First he picked up Yasmin's science book and showed it to Mr Gates. The inspector smiled at Yasmin. As he did, the door from the playground inched open and Jamal, Shea and the skeleton appeared. Everyone saw them, except for Mr Wellington and Mr Gates, who had their backs to the door.

"In here!" Jamal whispered. He opened the stationery cupboard and they pushed the skeleton

inside. A few seconds later, Shea came out and shut the door.

Mr Gates finished flicking through Yasmin's book. "Have you been using a model skeleton?" he asked. Yasmin glanced up at Mr Wellington.

"No," said the teacher.

"Doesn't the school have one?" asked Mr Gates.

"Well, actually we do…" started Mr Wellington.

Shea added. "Another class is using it. When they've finished, they're going to send it down."

"Good," said Mr Gates.

All the children were looking at the stationery cupboard.

"Have you been enjoying learning about bones?" Mr Gates asked Leon.

Mr Wellington whispered to Shea. "Where's Jamal?"

"He's in the stationery cupboard."

"What's he doing in the stationery cupboard?"

"He's fixing the skelington so you don't get into trouble."

Mr Wellington closed his eyes.

Then Mr Gates turned round. "You get on, Mr Wellington. I'm happy to fetch those lesson plans. Did you say they were in the stationery cupboard?"

"No!" said Mr Wellington. "I mean yes! But don't touch that door!"

"What do you mean?" asked Mr Gates.

"It's dangerous!" said Mr Wellington.

"How can a door be dangerous?"

"The whole cupboard could fall down at any moment," explained Mr Wellington. "Now time is ticking by and I suggest we get started."

The inspector looked at Mr Wellington as if he was as bonkers as a bag of baboons.

★★★

"Right, Purple Class," Mr Wellington announced, "I want you to open your books at the diagram of the skeleton you stuck in earlier." Science books rustled.

"Who remembers how many bones we have in our bodies?"

Ivette put up her hand. "206."

"Very good," said Mr Wellington. Then, as he spoke, he noticed Mr Gates turning round and reaching towards the handle of the stationery cupboard door.

"Mr Gates!" said Mr Wellington. "Shall we forget about the cupboard and get on with the lesson?" Mr Gates nodded. "All right," said Mr Wellington. "Now we're going to use these sticky labels to point to some bones you know about. I'm going to choose people to stick the labels on the…erm…"

Shea realized why he was stuck. "Mr Wellington needs the skelington," he whispered to Leon.

It was true. Mr Wellington needed the skeleton to teach the lesson. He scratched his head. Then he said, "Mr Gates, we wondered if you would mind joining in. We'd like you to stand on the carpet while the children stick labels on you."

"Stick labels on me?" said Mr Gates.

"Let's have a clap for Mr Gates," nodded Mr Wellington.

The children clapped and Mr Gates walked to the front.

"Where does this first one go?" asked Mr Wellington, holding up a label that said 'SKULL'. He gave it to Yasmin who stuck it, quite rightly, on Mr Gates's neck, pointing up at his head.

The next label said 'FEMUR', and Mr Wellington asked Jodie to stick it on. She walked up to Mr Gates and stuck it on his tie. "No," said Mr Wellington. "That's not a femur. Who can help?"

There was silence.

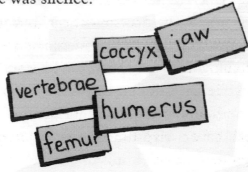

"Come on," said Mr Gates. "What's a femur?"

Leon put up his hand and said, "Isn't it a kind of motorbike?"

"No," said Mr Wellington, looking disappointed. "It's a leg bone!"

Jodie took the label off Mr Gates's tie and stuck it to his knee. Mr Gates breathed out loudly through his nose.

Then there was a knock at the door. It was a frizzy-haired girl from Orange Class called Danyelle. She walked straight in and said, "Excuse me, Mr Wellington. Miss Zanetos wants me to get some green paper from the stationery cupboard."

"Wait!" said Mr Wellington. "Be careful!"

"It's all right," nodded Danyelle, opening the stationery cupboard door.

Mr Wellington's mouth opened and closed. Mr Gates leaned round to look into the cupboard, and the 'SKULL' label fell on to the floor. Inside there seemed to be dust in the air. But there was no skeleton, and no Jamal.

"Thank you," said Danyelle, walking out with several large sheets of green paper.

Then there was another knock at the door.

"Yes!" called Mr Wellington.

To everyone's astonishment it was Jamal

wheeling the skeleton! What's more, every bone was where it was meant to be.

"Ah!" smiled Mr Gates. "That's what you need."

"The other class has finished with this," said Jamal.

"Thank you," said Mr Wellington.

***

From that moment on everybody was happy. Mr Gates pulled the label off his knee and looked through Mr Wellington's lesson plans. Mr Wellington finished the lesson, with the skeleton to help him. And the children did well at remembering the bones. (Except for Leon, who said he thought a fibula was someone who told lies.)

When Mr Gates finally left, it was nearly lunchtime. Mr Wellington looked around. "So who messed about with the skeleton this morning?" he asked. Jamal put up his hand. So did Zina and Shea. "Well I appreciate you being honest about it," said Mr Wellington, "but you are going to promise me you'll never do anything like that again."

Jamal, Zina and Shea all promised.

Then Ivette asked Jamal, "How come you went into the cupboard, but then you came in from the corridor?"

"When you're in a fix you've got to make smart moves," grinned Jamal. "I was trying to mend the skeleton. Then Mr Furlong started making a hole up above the cupboard. He said I had to go back into the classroom. I told him why I couldn't. So he said he'd help. He pulled me and the skeleton up through the ceiling and we used his tools to fix it. I told him all about the femur, the tibia and the fibula, and can I tell you the joke he told me?"

"As long as it's better than your usual jokes," said Mr Wellington.

"Why was the skeleton scared to go to the horror film?" Nobody knew. "Because it didn't have any guts," said Jamal.

The class groaned, but Mr Wellington rocked back in his chair and laughed so loudly that he didn't even hear the bell.

As Jamal headed off down the corridor there was a glint in his eye. It had been a good morning after all.

The Wild Area

The sky was clear blue above the playground and it felt hot, even though the day was only just starting. Mr Wellington had been off sick all week and, when he appeared, the children looked at each other with disappointed little nods and tuts.

"Are you better, Mr Wellington?" Leon asked, as they followed him to the classroom.

"I'm fine now, thank you, Leon," said Mr Wellington. "How have you been?"

"We had a supply teacher from America," Leon told him.

"Miss Brozinsky," said Ivette, in an American accent.

"She was the best teacher we've ever had," nodded Jodie.

"So everyone's had a good week," said Mr Wellington, leading them into the classroom.

"Mr Furlong hasn't had a good week," said Leon. "He fell down his ladder and landed on his rake."

"He broke it," pointed out Yasmin, "and he had to have his ankle x-rayed."

"Is he going to be all right?" asked Zina.

"I hope so," said Mr Wellington.

"So do I," added Leon, "because I like him. He's small like I am, and he calls everyone a silly old sausage."

Mr Wellington got out the register. Then he said, "Right! Blue Class is doing assembly in a few minutes. Then it's PE. So has everyone got their PE kits?"

Ivette put up her hand. "We don't call them 'PE kits' now," she said. "Since we had Miss Brozinsky we call them 'PE uniforms'."

"All right," sighed Mr Wellington, "but have you all got them?"

There was a "yes" from the carpet.

Then Jamal added, "And Miss Brozinsky said we need to have cookie breaks."

"Cookie breaks?" said Mr Wellington.

"It means we sit and eat cookies when we're tired," explained Jodie. "It's a very good system."

"Are we going to have cookie breaks with you?" asked Leon.

"I call them biscuits," said Mr Wellington, looking at the register.

"So let's call them 'Miss Brozinsky's biscuit breaks'," suggested Shea.

Mr Wellington wiggled his pen between his fingers. "If I give you lot 'Miss Brozinsky's biscuit breaks' whenever you're tired I'll get through about 450 packets of biscuits a week. So the answer is no."

There were groans from the carpet, which Mr Wellington ignored. He called the register and checked who was having packed lunches and who was having school dinners. Jodie put up her hand.

"What do you want, Jodie?" asked Mr Wellington.

"We don't call them 'packed lunches' now," she told him. "Since we had Miss Brozinsky we call them 'bag lunches'."

There was a murmur of agreement.

"Look," said Mr Wellington, "you can call them 'bag lunches', 'scrumptious, Miss Brozinsky's cookie-break munchkins' or 'one-eyed cats' for all I care. We've got to get this register done. Assembly is starting!"

***

Purple Class were the last ones to arrive in the hall and Leon could tell Mrs Sammy was cross.

"Come on, Purple Class!" she said.

They hurried in and, as soon as they sat down, the head-teacher picked up a box. Then she tipped it over. Drinks bottles, sweet wrappers and crisp packets fell on to the floor.

"This was in the playground!" said Mrs Sammy. "Mr Furlong hasn't been here to sweep up for two days and look at it all!" She looked at the children. "I'm happy to say that Mr Furlong will be back later this morning. But I don't want him to find the place covered in litter. So everyone's going to do some clearing up."

Each class was given a different part of the school to clean. Purple Class was put in charge of the Wild Area at the back of the playground.

Blue Class's assembly was all about the American West. They wore cowboy hats. They read a poem about buffaloes. They swung a lasso, and they ended by shouting, "YES, SIREEEE!"

After that Mrs Sammy looked a bit less cross. She thanked Blue Class. Then she held up a rake with a bright red handle. She said it was for Mr Furlong. She asked which class would like to welcome the caretaker back by presenting the rake to him at break. Lots of children from Purple Class threw up their hands, so Mrs Sammy gave the rake to Mr Wellington. He had to lift it over his head because everyone wanted to touch it on the way out of assembly. Outside, he said that one person was going to be in charge of presenting the rake. Then he looked around and chose Leon. Leon's smile was almost too big for his face.

"Shall I keep the rake until break, Leon?" Mr Wellington asked. "Or can you look after it safely yourself?"

"I'll look after it safely myself," said Leon.

Mr Wellington handed him the rake. "Be extra careful," he said, "and see if you can think of something nice to say to Mr Furlong when you present it to him."

"I'll think of something," said Leon, holding the rake proudly.

The Wild Area was a patch of bushes and trees with a pond in the middle, and most of the class liked going there. But as they came down the stairs, Jamal looked worried.

"Mr Wellington, I can't clear up the Wild Area because I've got new trainers. They're going to get ruined if I tread on mud."

"It's not muddy today," Mr Wellington told him.

"Well, they're going to get ruined if I tread on something else," said Jamal.

"Like what?"

"A hedgehog," suggested Jamal.

"Don't be daft," Mr Wellington told him. "You're quite happy to play football in those trainers."

"Well I definitely can't go," said Ivette.

Mr Wellington looked at her. "Why not, Ivette?"

"Because my mum's a beautician," she said.

"That's got nothing to do with it," said Mr Wellington.

"It has," said Ivette. "It means I don't like creepy-crawlies."

"Well, I shouldn't think creepy-crawlies like us very much," Mr Wellington told her.

They reached the bottom of the stairs and set off across the playground. Leon bounced Mr Furlong's rake on his small, square shoulders and, as they reached the gate into the Wild Area, he announced, "I've thought of something to say to Mr Furlong."

"What are you going to say?" asked Mr Wellington.

"Because we missed you and you are very funny we want to give you this small present."

"That would be fine," said Mr Wellington. Then children began pushing through the gateway in front of him. "Wait!" he called. "You're going to follow me quietly and sensibly along the path!"

★★★

When they reached the pond, Leon looked up at the trees and down at the water. You could see the bottom where sunbeams fell between the branches. Shea arrived, making quacking sounds like a duck and Ivette came behind him with her arms folded across her chest.

"You all right, Ivette?" Mr Wellington asked.

"Miss Brozinsky would never make us do this," she said.

"There's nothing to worry about," said Mr Wellington.

"There is," said Ivette. "Slugs."

Mr Wellington scratched his head. Jamal looked down at his feet.

"I'm not getting slugs on my trainers," he said.

"They suck your blood if you touch one," nodded Shea. "I saw it on TV."

"They don't," said Mr Wellington. "Slugs are completely harmless."

"How do you know?" asked Jodie.

"Because I've touched slugs before," said Mr Wellington.

The children looked at Mr Wellington as

though he had told them he had a bath in baked beans every night before he went to bed.

"That's gross big-time!" said Ivette.

"ANYWAY," went on Mr Wellington, "fortunately we didn't come here to save the world from killer slugs, or to tread on hedgehogs. We came here to clear up."

He took out a roll of bin bags. He split the class into teams and he gave each team a bag. Then he told them, "We're going to see which team can put the most litter in their bag."

Leon laid Mr Furlong's rake by the pond and joined his team as they hurried off picking up empty drinks cans, plastic wrappers and old bits of cardboard. Jamal found a mushroom. Zina found a football boot full of earth. Jodie asked if she could pick flowers for her mum. Mr Wellington told her she could smell the flowers but not pick them.

"This one smells like the stuff my dad puts under his arms," said Ivette.

Soon all the litter had been picked up. Zina's team had the heaviest bag, mainly because of the football boot full of earth.

Mr Wellington was starting to collect up the bags when Shea called out, "Look! Mr Furlong!"

Leon and the others turned round. The

caretaker's red van was pulling up by the side-entrance to the school.

Mr Wellington looked at Leon. "It'll be break time soon," he said. "Where's that rake?"

"Just there!" said Leon, with an excited nod.

Leon ran towards the pond, but he didn't see the rake in the grass and he stepped on one end of it. It flicked up into the air, flipped over and landed with a splosh in the middle of the pond. And there it stood.

The children stared.

"Oh, Leon," sighed Mr Wellington. "How did you manage to do that?"

Leon squeezed his lip between his fingers. "I can't give Mr Furlong his rake if it's in the pond," he said.

"Well, we'll find a way to sort this out," sighed Mr Wellington.

He put a foot in the shallowest part of the pond. But it was softer than he expected and he slipped. There was a cackle of laughter and a slurp of mud as Mr Wellington pulled his shoe out.

"You put your foot in it that time!" said Shea.

"Yes, Shea," said Mr Wellington grimly. "Now let's just stop and think about this."

But the children had ideas of their own. They circled the pond. Shea tried to prod the rake with a long stick, but the stick snapped. Zina tried throwing a fir cone at it, but the fir cone hit Ivette on the foot.

Mr Wellington told them all to stop. "Listen!" he said. "We're not going to get the rake back by flapping about like a lot of seagulls round a bag of chips. We're going to have to be clever about this."

"We could build a boat," said Zina, raising her eyebrows.

Mr Wellington shook his head.

"What about making a rope bridge out of string?" suggested Jamal.

Mr Wellington shook his head again.

Then Leon's eyes lit up. "We could empty the water out of the pond," he said.

"How?" asked Ivette.

"With the paint-pots from the classroom," Leon suggested.

This time it was Shea who shook his head. He said, "I think the only thing might be to call Air-Sea Rescue."

Mr Wellington took a long breath. Then he told the class, "I think the only thing might be to leave the rake there and tell Mr Furlong we're sorry."

Leon flapped his arms in the air. "I've gone and messed it all up," he groaned.

Then Yasmin put up her hand. "We could borrow Blue Class's lasso," she suggested.

There was a moment's silence.

"It's the best idea so far!" nodded Zina.

Mr Wellington looked at Yasmin. "Well, there'd be no harm in trying," he said.

So he sent Leon running across to Blue Class.

★★★

A few minutes later, Leon was back.

"He got it!" smiled Yasmin.

"Yes siree!" yelled Zina.

A discussion broke out about who should do the lassoing. Jamal said it should be him because he was the best at football. Ivette suggested they call Miss Brozinsky because she was American. But Mr Wellington took the lasso and said he was going to throw it himself.

"Do you want me to get a cowboy hat for you?" asked Leon.

"Don't worry, Leon," Mr Wellington told him.

The children stared as their teacher started swinging the loop of the lasso in a lopsided circle above his head.

"You just throw quickly and pull," said Ivette.

"And you say YEEHAW!" added Jamal.

Mr Wellington stared at the rake. He looped the lasso round four or five times more. Then he let go. The rope flew across the pond in exactly the right direction. But it was too high. Instead of going round the handle of the rake it caught on a branch of one of the trees.

"YEEHAW!" said Jamal.

"I knew you were going to miss," said Ivette.

Mr Wellington gave the rope a tug, but the loop didn't come off the branch, it tightened. He tried pulling from a different angle but that was even worse.

"Now it's stuck!" said Leon.

Everyone stared at the rake, and Mr Wellington put his hands on his hips.

"The bell's about to go for break," said Jodie.

"There's nothing more we can do," sighed Mr Wellington.

The rope trailed down from the branch to the

edge of the pond. Leon took hold of it and gave it a tug. "I could swing across and grab the rake," he said.

"No, Leon," said Mr Wellington.

"I'm a natural-born rope swinger," said Leon. "I do it at gymnastics club."

"You should let him," said Jamal.

"It's not even dangerous," said Leon. "You have to grab the rope high up."

He gave a little jump and gripped the rope. But he jumped higher than he meant to. When he tried to stop himself, his feet just scraped the ground.

"LEON!" called Mr Wellington, reaching out a hand. But it was too late. With eyes as wide as a frog's, Leon flew out across the pond.

"Grab the rake!" called Ivette.

Leon tried. But he was swinging too much to one side.

"HOLD ON!" called Mr Wellington.

Leon reached the far side of the pond. Then he started coming back. This time he was heading straight for the rake. He opened his mouth, kicked out a leg and got a hand on the rake all at the same time. There was a huge cheer from the children. The rake rose out of the water. Leon swung on. Then he completely lost his grip on the rope. The cheer became a gasp and Leon crashed into the water with an enormous splash.

Mr Wellington strode straight into the pond reaching out his hand. Leon stood up with mud all over one arm. But he was smiling because he was still holding the rake. Mr Wellington grabbed one end and pulled Leon on to the grass.

"Sorry," said Leon looking down at his shoes. "I promise I didn't want that to happen."

"I promise I didn't want that to happen either," said Mr Wellington.

★★★

Nobody really understood why Leon was wearing his PE kit when he led Mr Furlong into the

43

playground at break, nor why Mr Wellington had wet trousers and bare feet. But Mr Furlong was very pleased to get such a warm welcome back.

Mrs Sammy told him the school had bought him a little present. Then Leon held out the rake and said, "Because we missed you and you are very small we want to give you this funny present."

Everyone laughed but it didn't seem to matter. Mr Furlong liked the rake, and he made all the children laugh again when he turned to Mrs Sammy and said, "You shouldn't have bothered, you silly old sausage."

When it was over there were still a few minutes of break left.

"Do you want to play football with us, Mr Wellington?" asked Leon.

"Not today," said Mr Wellington. "I think I'm going to have a cookie break."

Slinkypants, the Crazy Snake

Jodie and Zina came in early from break. Jodie had a grass stain on the sleeve of her 'It's hard being a princess' t-shirt and she wanted to rinse it. Mr Wellington was still in the classroom. The children had been painting self-portraits and he was hanging them up with clothes-pegs.

"What's this treat we're going to have today?" Jodie asked him.

"I'll explain after break," said Mr Wellington. "But I can promise it will be nice and relaxing."

"I'm already nice and relaxed," said Jodie, turning on the tap and holding her sleeve underneath it. "Last night all I did was lie on my dad's recliner armchair and eat a box of chocolates."

"Very energetic, Jodie," said Mr Wellington, stepping back to look at the string of paintings.

"I need to renew my energy," said Jodie.

"I see," nodded Mr Wellington. "Well I hope you don't need to eat a *whole* box of chocolates to renew your energy."

"Chocolate is good for you, you know," said Zina. "It's made from cocoa, milk and sugar, and those are all a hundred percent natural ingredients."

"It's almost a salad," added Jodie.

Then the bell rang and Mr Wellington went to fetch the others.

★★★

"Come and sit on the carpet!" Mr Wellington said.

Leon was bouncing a tennis ball, and he put his hand up as he sat down. "Mr Wellington, you told us after break you'd say what treat we're having."

"That's right, Leon," said Mr Wellington. "You all know it's November Fun-Day, and we're going to do something special."

"Can we have a burping competition?" asked Jamal.

"Grow up, Jamal," replied Mr Wellington. "It isn't November Act-Like-A-Nincompoop Day."

"I bet we're going on an outing," said Ivette.

"Not this year," Mr Wellington told her. "Some classes are going on outings, but we're staying here."

Jodie puffed out her cheeks. "If it's November Fun-Day then we ought to go on an outing," she sighed.

"Whenever we go on an outing Yasmin's sick on the coach," remarked Shea.

But Mr Wellington interrupted. "Well no one is going to be sick today, Shea, because we're not going anywhere. We've got a visitor coming... and he's a storyteller."

The children didn't look very excited by that.

"A storyteller is boring," said Jamal.

Mr Wellington shook his head. "It isn't going to be boring."

"That's what you told us last year when we went to the plastic bag factory," said Zina.

"I thought the plastic bag factory was interesting," said Mr Wellington.

"If it's Fun-Day we should be going to a theme park with roller-coasters and raft rides," said Jodie.

"And eat-as-much-as-you-like pancakes," added Zina.

"Well, I'd be sick on the coach if that was what we did," said Mr Wellington.

"I bet Red Class are going to a theme park," muttered Jodie.

"Red Class are going to the plastic bag factory," said Mr Wellington. "Now if you lot want to carry on grumbling, we can always cancel the storyteller. I've gone to a lot of trouble to organize this treat for you. But if all I get is a lot of faces as long as ironing boards we might as well do some numeracy.

There's a whole set of topics ready. All I've got to do is switch on the whiteboard."

"If you make us do numeracy it'll be the November Fun-Day from hell!" said Jodie.

"Look," sighed Mr Wellington. "I'm not making you do anything. I'm giving you a choice. We can have storytelling this morning and numeracy tomorrow, or we can start doing numeracy right now!"

"I'm not even coming to school after today," said Jodie. "I'm going to China. All I've got to do is learn Chinese."

"OK, let's forget all about the storyteller." said Mr Wellington. He switched on the interactive whiteboard. Triangles and numbers appeared at the front of the class. "You'll find this topic quite fun," he said, looking at the screen.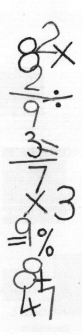

"Jodie," hissed Ivette. "Now look what you've gone and done?"

"I didn't really mean it, Mr Wellington," said Jodie.

Mr Wellington looked around the children's faces. "So you'd rather hear stories would you?"

The class nodded.

"All right," said their teacher. "But

remember, I can change my mind. If you keep this classroom calm, you can have your treat. If you can't manage that, we're doing numeracy. OK?" He switched off the whiteboard. Then he told them, "All right. I need to get to the office to see if the storyteller has arrived. I want you to tidy things up."

***

As Mr Wellington went out into the corridor, Leon took some paint-pots over to the sink. Yasmin went to put her 'Hooked on History' book into her tray. Jodie tried to squeeze some brushes into a pot and knocked over a box of blue powder paint. Then there was a scream. Heads turned. Yasmin was standing with her 'Hooked on History' book pressed against her mouth.

"There's a snake in my tray!" she said, breathlessly.

"It can't be a real, live snake," said Leon, looking into the tray.

But there was a snake. Its blotchy, brown coils were sliding across Yasmin's science book.

Other children hurried across. They clutched at each other's arms and tried to peer into Yasmin's tray. Shea said he was pretty sure it was a

snake that could kill you in a few seconds. Yasmin
said she was pretty sure she was going to be sick.
But before anyone could say anything else, the
snake gave a twist and raised its head out of the
tray. All the children stumbled back except for
Jodie, who was trying to get to the front.

"Oh no!" she groaned. "That's my dad's
snake. It's Slinkypants."

"Why did you put Slinkypants in Yasmin's
tray?" asked Ivette.

"He's not in Yasmin's tray any more," said
Jamal. "He's going into your tray, Ivette."

It was true. Slinkypants was slithering out of
Yasmin's tray and poking his head into Ivette's
tray.

"If it goes in there I'm totally going to die!"

exclaimed Ivette. "He's going to poison my pencil case or something!"

"Don't worry," said Jodie. "He's a corn snake. He's not even poisonous."

"I don't care," shouted Ivette. "How am I meant to get things out of my tray if there's a snake in there?"

"He doesn't do anything," Jodie told her. "My dad says he's as harmless as a canary."

"That doesn't mean you had to bring him to school," remarked Zina.

"I didn't mean to bring him!" said Jodie. "It's just that he escapes from his tank. Then he gets into my swimming bag because it's warm. I didn't know he was in it." She reached into her tray and tugged out a pink swimming bag. "He was in this," she said.

She pulled open Ivette's tray. Slinkypants was looking out with beady eyes.

Ivette turned down her mouth. "Where's my Groovy Chick gel pen gone?" she asked.

"Slinkypants must have eaten it," said Zina.

"Snakes don't eat gel pens," said Jodie.

"There's a bulge in Slinkypants," said Ivette, "and it looks like a gel pen to me."

"Shh! I think Yasmin's going to be sick," whispered Leon.

Jodie reached down and lifted Slinkypants out. The snake's little tongue licked the air and the children around Jodie gasped.

"It's all right," she said. "I have to pick him up all the time."

"Your Groovy Chick gel pen was underneath him," pointed out Zina.

"I don't even want that pen if a snake's touched it," snapped Ivette.

Slinkypants twisted around in Jodie's hands and Zina screwed up her face.

"You've got to take the snake to Mrs Sammy," said Jamal.

"Miss Sammy won't know what to do with a snake," said Jodie.

"She might scream and jump out the window," pointed out Leon.

"She's going to get angry," said Zina. "It's against school rules to bring snakes to school."

Jamal nodded. Then he added, "But if Mr Wellington comes back, I don't know what he'll do."

"Numeracy, probably," said Ivette.

Jodie unzipped her swimming bag. "I'm not going to tell Mr Wellington or Mrs Sammy," she said. " I'll just leave Slinkypants in this. Then I'll take him home and there won't be any trouble."

The snake gave a flick of his tail as Jodie put him carefully into the bag.

She did up the zip. But as she pushed the bag back into her tray, Leon said, "There's a hole!"

He was right. There was a hole in the bottom corner of the bag.

Jodie rolled her eyes. "That's how he got out in the first place."

"You've got to block it," said Jamal.

The children looked around for something to block the hole with.

"I'll get a clothes-peg!" said Jodie.

No one had time to agree or disagree. Everyone could hear Mr Wellington's voice. Jodie hurried across to the string with the self-portraits on. There was a clatter of feet and a scraping of chairs as the children scattered back to their places.

"Quickly!" hissed Shea, as Jodie darted back across the carpet.

She clipped a clothes-peg over the hole in the bag, pushed her tray shut and raced back to sit down.

"Look calm!" whispered Zina.

Everyone tried to. Ivette sucked her pencil. Jamal stared at the ceiling. Leon put his hands behind his head.

★★★

"This is Purple Class," said Mr Wellington, showing in a short man with curly hair and a big, green bag.

"Good morning, Purple Class," smiled the man.

"Good morning," said the class.

The storyteller took Mr Wellington's seat and asked the children to join him at the front.

"We're very lucky to have this special visitor," said Mr Wellington. "His name is Tonico Batucada. He comes all the way from Brazil. And I'd like you to give him a warm welcome."

The children clapped and Mr Wellington sat down on the carpet, next to the storyteller, with his back to the radiator.

"Thank you, Mr Wellington," said the storyteller. "And I am very delighted to see such bright eyes! So who knows anything about Brazil?"

"I do," said Jamal. "I'm the best at football and I can do at least five Brazilian ball tricks."

"Oh!" said Tonico Batucada, shaking Jamal's hand. "And are you really the best at football? Or are you the best at showing off?"

"It's not showing off," said Jamal. "It's a statistic.

Tonico Batucada laughed. Then he asked, "Who knows what language Brazilians speak?"

"Mexican!" called out Leon.

"No!" said the storyteller. "We speak Portuguese!"

Jodie gave a sideways glance at her tray. It looked completely normal.

"Well," said Tonico Batucada. "I'm sorry but I can't tell stories if everyone is being too calm and English! I think we have to start with some dancing. So stand up everyone and let me hear you clap!"

Everyone got to their feet. Tonico Batucada fished a tambourine, with ribbons on it, from his bag. Then he started tapping and bashing a rhythm. The ribbons danced and Jodie and the others clapped.

"That's very good!" said Tonico Batucada.

"Now move your feet back, forward, back like this!"

The children laughed and tried to move their feet like the storyteller.

Mr Wellington did it very quickly and the storyteller raised his eyebrows. "Now I know who's best at showing off in this classroom!" he said. "Let's hop!"

The whole class copied him, hopping on their left foot to the right, then on their right foot to the left.

"OK!" shouted the storyteller. "Now dance like Brazilians!"

His hips swished round and he did little taps and flips with his shoes. Jodie and Ivette were quite good at it. Leon was still hopping on his right foot to the left. Then Tonico Batucada slapped the tambourine and told them all to sit down. There was a lot of huffing and puffing and chatter.

"Listen!" said Tonico Batucada, and he launched into a story about a monkey that climbed into a garden to steal some bananas. It had everyone in fits of giggles. Then he told a spooky story about an old woman who was turned into a headless mule. She had fire coming out of her neck and, as the story got scarier, Tonico Batucada kept on making the children jump by saying, "THERE SHE IS! BEHIND YOU!"

In between the stories he taught the children some Portuguese. *Era uma vez* means 'Once upon a time', *obrigado* means 'thank you', and *saude* means 'bless you'.

Jodie was enjoying herself so much she forgot about Slinkypants. But, as Tonico Batucada started telling the next story, there was a little click. Jodie looked sideways and saw a clothes-peg on the floor by her tray. Worse still, Slinkypants' head was poking out of the hole in her bag.

★★★

Tonico Batucada didn't notice anything. He was busy describing how you have to walk in the rainforest when there are dangerous animals about. Jodie looked across again and saw Slinkypants slithering out of the bag, on to the radiator.

The snake's eyes glinted and the children stared in astonishment as it slid along the top of the radiator towards the storyteller. As it got closer, Shea could hardly contain himself. He started jigging his legs about with excitement.

"Will you stop wriggling around, Shea?" asked Mr Wellington. "You're making me seasick."

"But there's a snake right behind you, Mr Wellington!" Shea blurted out.

Tonico Batucada looked at Shea and nodded. "Mr Wellington and I are experts!" he smiled. "You won't trick us!"

Then the snake slipped off the radiator and landed on the side of Mr Wellington's head. None of the children had ever seen anyone with such a funny look on their face.

"Oh, my life!" shrieked Mr Wellington, flapping his arms, jumping to his feet and picking up a ruler to defend himself.

Shea kicked his legs in the air and roared with laughter as Slinkypants slithered sideways down the side of Mr Wellington's chair and dropped on to the carpet. Half the class screamed because the snake was coming towards them.

"Get back from it!" yelled Mr Wellington, pointing his ruler at the snake.

"It's OK," said Jodie, bending down. "He's my dad's pet!"

But Tonico Batucada beat her to it. He squatted down with an outstretched arm. Then he grabbed the snake by the back of its head.

It took Jodie several minutes to explain why Slinkypants had been on the radiator in Purple Class. Mr Wellington said she owed Tonico Batucada an apology.

"No worries!" said the storyteller, still with the snake in his hands. "I am used to snakes since I was a boy. But I would like to finish my story."

Jamal got a box from the stationery cupboard. Jodie put Slinkypants inside it, with a towel to keep him warm. Mrs Sammy arrived and stood by the sink talking to Jodie's dad on her mobile. Then Mr Furlong turned up and took the box away for safekeeping. At last, Tonico Batucada could carry on with his story about the rainforest.

When he finished, it was almost lunchtime and Mr Wellington said it would have to be the last story. The class groaned.

"Well," said Tonico Batucada. "Everything has an end. Except for a sausage... which has two ends!"

There was laughter and Mr Wellington told the storyteller, "I know Purple Class have really enjoyed having you here."

"*Obrigado,*" said Jodie.

"Not at all," smiled Tonico Batucada. "And listen. I know many schools round the world and I want to tell you something. You are lucky to have this teacher, Mr Wellington. He is a good one. Do you know that?"

The children nodded.

Shea said, "We'll sell him to you very cheaply if you want."

As Tonico Batucada picked up his green bag, Jodie told him, "I'm sorry about the snake."

"It was good," said Tonico Batucada. "Now I have a new story to tell in Brazil – the story of Purple Class and Slinkypants, the crazy snake!"

★★★

The bell went, Tonico Batucada left, and the children trailed after him on their way to lunch. Mr Wellington noticed a box of blue powder paint on its side and stood it upright. The powder made him sneeze, and a voice from the back of the class said, *"Saude!"*

It was Jodie, standing at the sink. She was having another go at washing the stain off her 'It's hard being a princess' t-shirt.

"Thank you, Jodie," said Mr Wellington.

"I'm sorry about all that," Jodie told him.

"Well, I know you didn't mean to bring a snake to school," said Mr Wellington. "But I'm not at all happy that you tried to keep it a secret. You should have told me straight away!"

Jodie nodded. Then she said, "You looked funny when Slinkypants fell on your head."

"Well, it is November Fun-Day," said Mr Wellington.

They both walked over to the door and Mr Wellington clicked off the lights.

"So are you still off to China then?" he asked.

"No," shrugged Jodie. "I'm going to Brazil."

Mr Wellington nodded. "All you've got to do is learn Portuguese."

"I've already made a start at that," said Jodie.

The Green Lady

The classroom was full of bustle. In the middle of it, Yasmin put her hands into the light of the slide projector. A shadow appeared on the wall. It looked like a crocodile. An eye bulged from its head. It even had a creepy sort of smile.

Yasmin glanced at Shea. The two of them were meant to be choosing a hand-shadow to do in Purple Class's Science-Week assembly, but Shea was more interested in throwing bits of cardboard at Jamal.

"This is good, Shea," said Yasmin quietly.

Shea looked at the wall and turned down his mouth. "I can do a better one," he said, putting his hands in front of hers.

Yasmin looked at Shea's hand-shadow.

"What's that?" she asked.

"A swan," said Shea.

"Looks more like a donkey!" said Jamal.

Yasmin reached out a hand and made two long ears on top of Shea's hand-shadow. Shea looked surprised.

"Do that in the assembly, Yasmin!" grinned Jamal.

"She won't dare," said Shea. "Yasmin's scared!"

"No, I'm not," said Yasmin.

"YES, YOU ARE!" shouted Shea, throwing his arms out to make her jump. "See! Chicken!"

Mr Wellington turned round. "Shea!" he called. "Did I ask you to start jumping about like an electric monkey?"

He was going to add something else but, before he could, there was an almighty crash. Leon had tripped over the slide projector's flex and dropped a tray of candles on to Jodie's head. Ivette tried not to laugh. Jodie tried not to cry.

Mr Wellington put a hand in the air and

shouted, "Right! Stop where you are! There's absolutely no need for all this hoo-hah! It's like being stuck in a telephone box with a brass band!"

The children froze.

"You're over excited," said Mr Wellington. "Now everybody come and sit on the carpet. Our assembly isn't until midday. There's no reason why anyone should be rushing about!"

The children shuffled across.

Mr Wellington folded his arms. "Now," he said, "someone remind me how we're going to start the assembly."

"I'm going to turn out the lights," said Jamal. "Then everyone's going to demonstrate things about light."

"That's right, Jamal," said Mr Wellington.

"I'm going to do the narrating with Ivette," said Zina.

"And I'm going to do a hand-shadow of a swan," said Shea.

"All right," said Mr Wellington. "What about you, Leon? What are you going to do with the tray of candles?"

Leon didn't look very sure.

"He'd better not drop it on my head again," said Jodie.

"He won't," said Mr Wellington. "He's going

to carry it in to demonstrate how light used to be made."

Leon bit his lip and said, "I don't want to carry the candles in any more.

"All right. You can turn on the slide projector, Leon. Someone else can carry the candles."

"Not me," said Zina. "If the lights are out it'll be spooky."

"The Green Lady is going to appear," nodded Ivette.

Mr Wellington frowned.

"Who's the Green Lady?" asked Jamal.

"She's a ghost in this school," said Ivette. "But no one knows if she's really real."

"She isn't," said Mr Wellington.

"She is," nodded Jodie. "My sister's friends saw her in the upstairs girls' toilets. You could only see her from the knees up and her face looked like it'd got rubber bands all over it."

"Sounds like my nan," said Jamal.

The whole class burst out laughing and Mr Wellington had to hold up his hand again.

"You're too old to believe in green ghosts!" he sighed. "Now who's going to carry in the candles?"

Yasmin looked around. Everyone was shaking their heads.

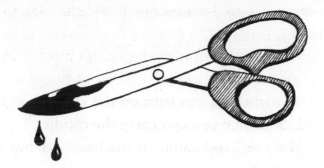

"There's no such thing as ghosts," said Mr Wellington firmly. "Even if there were, why on earth would one want to live in the girls' toilets at this school?"

"She used to be a teacher here," said Shea.

"Called Mrs Green," nodded Zina.

"Then she killed a First Year with a pair of scissors," added Shea.

"Ever since she's been trying to wash the blood off her hands in the basins."

"Anything else?" asked Mr Wellington, "Does she fly through the kitchens on a broomstick and cackle at the dinner ladies?"

"No," said Zina. "She's a ghost! Not a witch!"

"She makes a sign when she's going to appear," said Ivette.

"And she's got a wooden tail," added Jodie.

"Oh don't be so ridiculous!" said Mr Wellington.

Yasmin put up her hand. The class looked round and she could feel her face beginning to go red. "I'll carry the candles," she said.

"Thank you, Yasmin," said Mr Wellington. "At least one of you has got their head screwed on."

Shea stared at Yasmin. "The Green Lady's going to walk behind you and whisper 'I will haunt you from the cradle to the grave!'"

"Quiet!" snapped Mr Wellington.

"I don't even believe in the Green Lady," said Yasmin. "How could there have been a teacher who was green?"

Mr Wellington nodded. Just then there was a creak from the wet-break shelf. Slowly, all the games and puzzles tumbled on to the floor. Cards fluttered about and tiddlywinks came rolling across the carpet.

"It's the Green Lady's sign!" said Jodie.

"It means she's going to appear," said Zina.

"It means whoever put those games back did a lousy job of it!" said Mr Wellington. He was about to add something else when there was a soft knock at the door.

"It's her!" said Shea, making his eyes go wide.

The whole class looked round. There was another knock. This time even softer.

"She's very polite, this Green Lady," said Mr

Wellington. "I thought ghosts just walked through the wall." Then he called out, "Come in!"

There was silence.

"I SAID COME IN!"

***

The door opened slowly, and two children from Orange Class appeared. One of them was a short boy in glasses. The other was a girl with long, fair hair.

"Oh," said Mr Wellington, "Good morning, Alvin. Good morning, Estelle. Is it just you two or is there a woman out there with rubber bands on her face?"

Estelle looked over her shoulder. "Mrs Sammy's down the corridor," she said, "but I don't think she's got rubber bands on her face."

The children on the carpet started laughing.

Alvin took a deep breath. Then he said, "Sorry to disturb you, but Miss Zanetos is ill so we've got a supply teacher and she asked us to ask Mrs Sammy something and Mrs Sammy asked us to ask you.

"I see," said Mr Wellington. "And what exactly did your supply teacher ask you to ask Mrs Sammy that Mrs Sammy asked you to ask me?"

"Where are you going to do your Science-Week assembly?"

"In the upstairs hall," said Mr Wellington. "And it's going to feature the Green Lady playing the bagpipes with paper clips on her ears."

Alvin nodded.

"Thank you Mr Wellington," said Estelle and they walked off.

"That was a silly thing to say, Mr Wellington," said Jodie.

"Yes, it was!" he replied. "Just like the fuss you lot have been making for the past twenty minutes. Now, we've worked hard on this assembly. Let's not spoil it!" He stood up. Then he said, "Yasmin, I'm going to ask you, Shea and Jamal to start taking things upstairs. The rest of us will tidy up down here."

★★★

Yasmin, Shea and Jamal cut across the empty playground. The sky was grey and the breeze blew Yasmin's hair about. Jamal pushed open the door at the bottom of the stairs up to the hall. It was quiet. There was a smell of floor-polish and wet shoes.

"Spooky," said Shea, looking up the stairs.

Yasmin walked up the first steps.

"What's that sound?" asked Jamal.

"Don't be stupid!" said Yasmin.

But there was a sound: a funny sort of scraping and swishing.

"It's the Green Lady, sharpening her scissors," whispered Shea.

"Someone is coming!" said Jamal.

The swishing sound came closer.

"Shhh," whispered Yasmin.

Then round the corner appeared Alvin, Estelle and other children from Orange Class. They were dragging a PE mat.

"We're doing PE outside because you're in the hall," explained Estelle.

"Is the Green Lady really going to play bagpipes in your assembly with paper clips on her ears?" asked Alvin.

"Yes!" nodded Shea. "She's going to make your liver quiver and your knees freeze."

The boys hurried up the stairs, trying not to laugh. Near the top was the corridor that led through to the upstairs toilets. As Yasmin went past, it gave her an uneasy sort of feeling. Jamal and Shea stopped.

"Let's see you go in the girls' toilets then, Yasmin."

"Why?" she asked.

"Because you said you don't believe in the Green Lady," nodded Shea.

"I don't."

"Then go on."

Yasmin shook her head.

"See!" smirked Shea. "Chicken!"

Yasmin looked at him with her big, dark eyes. Then she said, "All right. You watch. You're the ones who are chicken."

***

Yasmin put down the things she was carrying and walked down the corridor. Halfway along was the door into the toilets.

"Whoooooo!" came a ghostly sound from behind her, but she knew who was making that.

The door was stiff as though it hadn't been opened for weeks. The lights were off. To one side Yasmin could make out the basins. To the other

side was the line of toilet cubicles. There was a hissing sound coming from one of the taps.

Yasmin's hand touched the cool wall tiles, feeling for the light switch. She couldn't find it. As she ran her hand up and down the wall a gust of wind came through a little window high in the wall. Then there was a creak. The door of one of the cubicles was closing.

"Hello?" Yasmin said. Then her hand hit the light switch and the bulb above her flickered on.

Two of the doors into the cubicles were open. But the end one was swinging, very slowly, shut. As she watched, it closed with a click. Yasmin could feel her heart beating. She stepped towards the closed door and suddenly she had a feeling that there was someone behind it. She bent down to look under the door. And, all at once, there was a screech from behind her. It was the door from the corridor opening. She swung round. There was a hand holding it open and it wasn't Shea's hand or Jamal's.

It was Mr Wellington's. "Yasmin?" said his voice from outside.

"I was just…" she said hurrying back to the door.

"I know exactly what you were doing," said Mr Wellington. "Honestly, Yasmin. I sent you up because I thought you'd be sensible! Now you've got the whole class worked up!"

Yasmin wasn't used to being told off. The rest of the class was waiting on the stairs and Mr Wellington carried on up to the hall.

"Did you see anything?" Ivette whispered.

"No," Yasmin replied, "but there was a noise from the end cubicle."

"Quiet!" snapped Mr Wellington, looking back over his shoulder.

"That's where my sister's friend saw her!" whispered Jodie.

"Jodie!" said Mr Wellington. "What are ears for?"

"For wearing earrings?" said Jodie, and the whole class burst into giggles.

But Mr Wellington didn't laugh. "Look, you lot!" he said. "Are we going to do this assembly or not?" He stared at their faces. Most of them nodded. "Well, how can we do it if everyone's chit-chattering about ghosts? Personally I don't care if Yasmin saw the Green Lady doing a handstand in the basins, waving her wooden tail out of the window! We've got work to do!"

The children nodded again, and Mr Wellington led them into the hall. "It's like trying to nail porridge to the wall, getting you lot to do an assembly," he sighed. "Now get in your positions. We're going to do a run through."

Zina and Ivette stood by the microphone. Leon got ready to turn on the slide projector. Yasmin waited outside. Mr Wellington pulled down the blinds. Then, when everyone was ready, he came out and lit the candles on the tray.

"Shea," he said. "You open the doors for Yasmin when Zina says, 'In the old days there were no electric lights so people used candles...'." Shea nodded. "Right!" called Mr Wellington. "Lights out!"

The hall went dark. There was a moment's silence.

Then Zina started. "Welcome to Purple Class's Science-Week assembly. Our assembly is all about 'Light and Shadow'..."

Shea got ready to open the doors. Yasmin was about to pick up the tray of flickering candles.

Then something moved behind her. She looked round, and what she saw chilled her down to her bones.

There was an old woman in a green dress gliding out of the darkness. It was like a terrible dream. Yasmin gazed as the figure raised its head and stared at her. She could barely see its face. But she knew it was someone she'd never seen in the school before. The eyes stared into hers for a moment. Then the figure glided back into the darkness. Yasmin wanted to scream. But Shea beat her to it.

"Aaaaaaaaah!" he yelled, flying through the door into the hall.

★★★

Jodie put her hands over her head. Leon switched on the slide projector. Zina ran into Jamal. And Mr Wellington rushed over to turn on the lights.

"WHAT ON EARTH IS GOING ON?" he asked.

Shea told him about the figure on the stairs.

"All right," said Mr Wellington, letting up one of the blinds. "If someone was on the stairs it must have been a teacher."

"But it was a horrible old woman," blurted out Shea. "She was in a green dress and she had a wrinkly face."

"It was probably Mrs Sammy," said Mr Wellington in his calmest voice.

But Leon shook his head. "It wasn't! Look! Mrs Sammy's in the playground and she's wearing brown trousers!"

Everyone looked down.

"Well, where's Yasmin?" asked Mr Wellington. He looked round, but Yasmin wasn't there.

"Yasmin?" called Shea.

"The Green Lady's got her!" whispered Zina.

"Nobody's got her," said Mr Wellington, striding towards the doors. "This is a school, not a haunted house!"

There was an eerie sight at the top of the stairs. The candles were flickering on the tray, but there was no sign of Yasmin.

"Yasmin?" called Mr Wellington.

There was no reply.

"Look in the toilets!" said Ivette.

Mr Wellington puffed out his cheeks. "Yasmin?" he said again, walking slowly down the corridor to the toilets.

Yasmin wasn't in the toilets. In fact she was almost at the bottom of the stairs. When Shea had gone running into the hall she had set off after the green figure. Now she could hear slow footsteps just ahead of her and, as she turned the corner, there was the green figure in front of her.

"Excuse me!" said Yasmin.

The woman in green turned round. She had cold eyes. Her face was old, though not as old as Yasmin had expected. Then something completely unexpected happened. Estelle and Alvin appeared

on the stairs. Yasmin didn't know quite what to feel.

"You're not the Green Lady are you?" she asked.

"The who?" replied the old woman.

Alvin pushed his glasses up his nose and said, "This is our supply teacher, Mrs Haynes."

"Oh," said Yasmin.

"Are you ready for us to come up to assembly now?" asked Estelle. "We've been waiting."

"No," smiled Mrs Haynes. "I popped up and Purple Class are still rehearsing."

At that moment Mr Wellington appeared with the rest of the class behind him.

"I can explain everything," said Yasmin. And she did.

***

There was no time to practise the assembly. But it worked out all right. The only slight hitch was at the start. Jamal turned out the lights. Yasmin walked in with the candles, and all the children in Orange Class started singing, *Happy birthday to you...* The rest went fine. Zina and Ivette remembered what they were supposed to say. Mr Wellington shone a torch and made a shadow of

Jodie on the wall. Leon switched on the slide projector at the right moment. And there was a surprise right at the end.

It was Shea's hand-shadow of a swan. It had improved. It looked quite like a real swan. But, as it went gliding along the wall, a fierce-looking crocodile shadow suddenly appeared and swallowed it. There was laughter and a round of applause. In the darkness, nobody was sure who had made the crocodile hand-shadow. But there was one person in Purple Class who knew!

Watch out for
more Purple Class adventures
in Autumn 2006!

For over fifteen years Sean Taylor
has worked as a visiting author and storyteller
in schools, encouraging children to write
poems and stories. The Purple Class stories spring
directly from those visits and all the dramas and funny
things he sees going on in classrooms. Sean spends
a lot of his life in Brazil, where he is quite often asked
to tell stories in Portuguese. The strangest invitation
was to tell British ghost stories at the Werewolf
Festival at a small town called São Luís do Paraitinga.
There was a howling competition in the town
square! If Sean could be one character from
the Purple Class stories, he says he'd probably
be Slinkypants, the crazy snake.

Butter-Finger

Bob Cattell and John Agard
Illustrated by Pam Smy

Riccardo Small may not be
a great cricketer – he's only played twice before
for Calypso Cricket Club – but he's mad
about the game and can tell you the averages of every
West Indies cricketer in history. His other love
is writing calypsos. Today is Riccardo's chance to make
his mark with Calypso CC against The Saints.
The game goes right down to the wire with captain,
Natty and team-mates, Bashy and Leo
striving for victory, but then comes the moment
that changes everything for Riccardo...

ISBN 10: 1-84507-376-2
ISBN 13: 978-1-84507-376-3

The Great Tug of War

Beverley Naidoo
Illustrated by Piet Grobler

Mmutla the hare is a mischievous trickster.
When Tswhene the baboon is vowing to throw you off
a cliff, you need all the tricks you can think of!
When Mmutla tricks Tlou the elephant
and Kubu the hippo into having an epic tug of war,
the whole savanna is soon laughing at their
foolishness. However small animals should not make
fun of big animals and King Lion sets out
to teach cheeky little Mmutla a lesson...

These tales of Mmutla's tricks,
are the African origins of America's beloved stories
of Brer Rabbit. Their warm humour and lovable
characters are guaranteed to enchant
new readers of all ages.

ISBN 10: 1-84507-055-0
ISBN 13: 978-1-84507-055-7

Hey Crazy Riddle!

Trish Cooke

Illustrated by Hannah Shaw

Why does Agouti have no tail?
How did Dog lose his bone?
Why can't Wasp make honey?

Find the answer to these
and other intriguing questions in this collection
of vivid and melodic traditional tales from
the Caribbean. Sing along to these stories as you
discover how Dog sneaks into Bull's party,
why Cockerel is so nice to Weather no matter
whether she rains or shines, and if the dish
really ran away with the spoon!

ISBN 10: 1-84507-378-9
ISBN 13: 978-1-84507-378-7

Coming in August 2006

Christophe's Story

Nicki Cornwell

Illustrated by Karin Littlewood

Christophe is a young
Rwandan asylum seeker, now living in the UK
with Mama and Papa. Christophe is having trouble
getting used to his new school, new language
and new life. Christophe is still learning English
so he struggles with the work that Miss Finch
gives the class. Most of all he misses his grandfather
who they had to leave behind. When a group
of boys discover a scar on Christophe's chest made
by a bullet from the gun of a Rwandan soldier,
Christophe bravely decides to share
his story with his classmates – so he tells them
of the terrifying day the soldiers
came to his house…

ISBN 10: 1-84507-521-8
ISBN 13: 978-1-84507-521-7

Roar, Bull, Roar!

Andrew Fusek Peters and Polly Peters

A year abroad for Czech brother
and sister Jan and Mari means arriving in rural
England in the middle of the night –
and not everyone is welcoming. As they try
to settle into their new school, they are plunged into
a series of mysteries. Who is the batty old lady
in the tattered clothes? Why is their new landlord such
a nasty piece of work? What is the real story
of the ghostly Roaring Bull – and what lies hidden
in the local church? Old legends are revived
as Jan and Mari unearth shady secrets in
a desperate bid to save their family from eviction.
In their quest, they find unlikely allies
and deadly enemies: enemies who will stop
at nothing to keep the past buried.

ISBN 10: 1-84507-520-X
ISBN 13: 978-1-84507-520-0

Dear Whiskers

Ann Whitehead Nagda
Illustrated by Stephanie Roth

Everyone in Jenny's Class has to write
a letter to someone in another class. Only you have
to pretend you are a mouse! Jenny thinks
the whole thing is really silly... until her pen friend
writes back. There is something mysterious
about Jenny's pen friend. Will Jenny
discover her secret?

"This warm story with a positive message
will make a great choice for newly independent
readers, as a read-aloud, and as
a wonderful introduction to a letter-writing unit."
School Library Journal

ISBN 10: 1-84507-563-3
ISBN 13: 978-1-84507-563-7